# The Jungle Was Too Quiet...

Calm down, she told herself. You're imagining things.

Unfortunately, telling yourself that you're only imagining things, doesn't help you with things that are real. The tiny legs creeping across her neck were that kind of real. Shanzi tried not to scream, held her breath, and quickly reached for the thing at her neck, tossing it to the ground.

The scalpel spider had fallen on its back and was desperately trying to right itself, its legs waving madly. Each of those eight legs ended in razor-sharp barbs. If any had pierced her skin, so far from home, Shanzi knew she was as good as dead. Her hand shaking, she reached around and felt her neck where the spider had landed and pulled her hand back. There was no blood.

She was okay.

# TALES FROM THE WONDER ZONE

## Stardust

## Explorer

## Orbiter

More Science Fiction
from Trifolium Books Inc.

**Packing Fraction
& Other Tales of Science
and Imagination**

# Explorer

Edited by
## Julie E. Czerneda

Illustrated by
## Jean-Pierre Normand

**Trifolium Books Inc.**
Toronto, Canada

We acknowledge the financial support of the Government of Canada through the Book Publishing Industry Development Program (BPIDP) for our publishing activities.

**Canadian Cataloguing in Publication Data**
 Main entry under title:
  Explorer
 (Tales from the wonder zone)
 ISBN 1-55244-022-2
 1. Children's stories, Canadian (English) 2. Children's stories, American.
 3. Science fiction, Canadian (English) 4. Science fiction, American.
 I. Czerneda, Julie, 1955– II. Normand, Jean-Pierre III. Series.

 PS8323.S3E96 2002    jC813'.08762089282    C00-931741-4
 PZ5.E96 2002

Trifolium Books Inc.
250 Merton Street, Suite 203,
Toronto Ontario M4S 1B1
info@trifoliumbooks.com   www.trifoliumbooks.com

Cover Design and Illustrations: Jean-Pierre Normand
Text Design: John Lee, Heidy Lawrance Associates

Printed in Canada
9 8 7 6 5 4 3 2 1

## Dedications

**Julie E. Czerneda:** To Jim Rogerson and all the others at Trifolium Books for taking on this venture. To the contributors and their wonderful imaginations. To C. J. Cherryh, with special thanks for her introduction to this book. And to Jean-Pierre, who once again worked his magic.

**Jean-Pierre Normand:** To my parents, Marcel Normand and Bernadette Morin, who made it all possible for me.

**Derwin Mak:** To my parents Adrian and Georgette, for waking me up to watch Apollo 11; to my sister Christine for introducing me to science fiction; and to Julie Czerneda, for asking me to write.

**Pat York:** To my husband James York for his support.

**Marcel Gagné:** When I was asked for a dedication for this story, one person came immediately to mind because she is *always* in my thoughts. That one person is Sally Tomasevic, my wife, partner, and best friend in this universe.

**Isaac Szpindel:** To my family and friends, and especially my wife, Michelle, and our children, Aliya, Jaron, and Gavriel. You are the source of my wonder and of this story.

**James Alan Gardner:** Sincere thanks to Mrs. Gordon, Mrs. Stewart, Mrs. Fallis, Mrs. Coutts, Mrs. Durward, Mr. Fairbairn, and Mrs. Bent: the public school teachers who taught me to read.

# CONTENTS

## A Special Introduction by C.J. Cherryh

We all arrive as strangers to this planet, just a single second old and in a foreign place. We don't know then where we are or who we are, where we came from or where we're going tomorrow. That's our job to find out.

Some of us become content with: "This is my family, this is my town, this is the way things are."

But some others of us love asking questions, and keep looking for new things. We do what explorers do when they're in a strange place — we climb up high and look over the fences and over the towns and beyond the hills that seemed like the edge of the world. We take a look from the highest, most different place we can find and discover that the path we thought was just kind of crooked and winding for no reason at all goes around this most marvelous little pond, and that this fork of the trail leads back home, but the other one leads to another house, where this girl is sitting wishing for something interesting to happen.

The view from higher up can show us things that we haven't seen before.

That's what science fiction does. It gives us a different way of looking at things — a different way of looking at ourselves. It's a way of being a different size or a different color or a very different person for a while, and coming back and looking at all you know and asking yourself, with a little wider understanding, "Do I really know enough?" or "Might there be something else?"

Science fiction — really good science fiction — isn't all about creatures from outer space. It's about that sense of discovery and exploration that tingles through you when you know there are new things to find. It's that special look from a higher place. It's that feeling you get when you're about to open a box all done up in holiday wrapping. It's that feeling you get when you look up in the darkest night and see the Moon and wonder what it's like to be a kid two hundred years from now looking down at an Earth you've never visited.

It's called "sense of wonder." It's that other important question, right along with "why?"

It's "what if?"

That's what science fiction is about. And whatever story provokes that kind of feeling is, in a way, science fiction. The stories about Odysseus and his voyages, Sindbad the Sailor...those are very old science fiction stories. But new science fiction stories might be about voyages, or medicine, or the way nature works, or about discovering something unsuspected about ourselves. It's not about what was — it's about what might be.

All through the history of the world until now, there have been some places on this planet where no human being ever walked. Those places are getting scarcer and scarcer. Most of the unvisited places still left are on the tops of the highest mountains and the bottoms of the oceans. That means a problem for the young — a lack of places to go — a scarcity of things to imagine. It can make a young person think there's nothing left to explore.

But listen. Once upon a time there was a prince named Alexander. History would someday call him Alexander the Great, but when he was a boy he was just Alexander, and his father was Philip, who was a king. One day Alexander's teacher found him with tears in his eyes, because King Philip had done so much Alexander feared there would be nothing in the world left for him to do.

That was long before Alexander took his own journey to lands his father had never imagined existed. This is a true story, but it might have been science fiction.

Look up at night. Look at all those suns...yes, stars are suns!...and know that astronomers have already discovered planets circling no few of them. There are whole new solar systems out there...not to mention the galaxies.

Think that somewhere up there, a very different person might be looking up at one very tiny dim dot: a star, but not just any star. This dot is your Sun at a great distance. Think how this person might wonder if your Sun has planets. Could this stranger ever in his wildest dreams imagine anyone like you? What would you each do if you knew about each other?

Wonder. Imagine. Discover. The universe is wider than the wisest, oldest human being on Earth has ever measured. It's more detailed than the smallest living things on this planet and bigger than our telescopes can measure. I know a place where two suns are so close they constantly trade rivers of fire. I know a place where ice covers an entire world. I know a place where a prince is buried and no one has ever found him.

You're all Alexander. And the worlds you have to discover haven't even been imagined yet.

*C.J. Cherryh*

C.J. Cherryh is the award-winning author of numerous science fiction and fantasy titles, including the Cyteen, Chanur, and Foreigner series.

# The Snow Aliens

## by Derwin Mak

**W**ill Lawrence sucked in the cold air, blew it back out, and watched his breath form a miniature cloud. As the cloud faded, he looked up and saw a much larger cloud hovering above the field. Then he looked at the field. In the summer, it would have been full of corn. Now, in the winter, it was barren except for snow —

— and two tiny aliens, both the size of a period on a printed page.

"The meteorologist says it'll snow again," he said, pointing at the cloud.

1

Captain Susan McNaughton shivered in her Air Force coat. "If it snows again, the aliens will get buried. I hope their ship picks them up soon."

It had seemed like a fun idea to Tonn. Why not float in the atmosphere of the planet of giants, the blue third planet of the yellow sun? The planet was as large as home and had the same gravity, but its creatures, especially the dominant *Homo sapiens* species, were gigantic. Going down to the planet could be dangerous, even if the *Homo sapiens* had promised they would welcome Tonn and his crew in peace. Better to float in the air and collect atmospheric data there.

"But Tonn, why do you have to go outside the ship?" Ziv had said. "Our probes can collect the data."

"It is more fun to go outside — to feel the coolness of the alien wind and the heat of the yellow sun," Tonn had answered.

Soon, against the advice of his crew, Tonn jumped through the hatch, followed by Ziv.

"I am coming to keep you out of trouble," she muttered.

Tonn's carapace glowed orange with happiness as he floated in the air. He bounced around as the air currents tossed him up and down. As he waved at Ziv through the wispy clouds, he saw globes of water and chunks of dust sail past him.

4

"Hydrogen and oxygen together — water," he said, looking at his scanner. "These clouds are gaseous water floating in an atmosphere of carbon dioxide and oxygen. And there are numerous water particles floating here, too. This planet has lots of water, so much that it floats into the atmosphere. Not like home, where the water stays as liquid on the ground."

"We could have learned all this from inside the ship," said Ziv.

A globe of water sailed into Tonn and splashed all over him. He turned orange again and drifted away from Ziv.

"Tonn, do not go so far away from the ship!" she yelled.

Tonn shot a stream of hydrogen from his backpack and flew into Ziv's arms. Ziv flashed green with anger and slapped him with all four claws.

"Tonn, stop playing!" she ordered. "Get your data so we can go back to the ship."

Tonn drifted into a wisp of cloud. He had never felt so free; he felt as if he could stay outside and float forever.

But then he felt the wind get colder. The clouds became thicker. The globes of water began to turn white. One flew into him. Instead of splashing, it bounced off his carapace.

The water is becoming solid, he thought. He looked around. He couldn't see through the clouds anymore, and more ice chunks began speeding around him.

"Ziv! Ziv!" he yelled. "Where are you?"

Ziv grabbed him from behind. "We must go back," she said.

"I cannot see the ship," said Tonn. The clouds had turned from wispy gases into a big white mass.

New objects floated in the air: large white stars formed from triangles, hexagons, and circles etched with beautiful patterns. No two stars were alike. Millions of them appeared from nowhere. Then the stars began to fall.

At first Tonn thought the stars might be intelligent creatures, but he saw two of them collide and split into globes of water.

"The stars are water," he said. "What strange phenomenon... "

He remembered the TV signals from the *Homo sapiens*. "They have a semisolid form of water," he said. "They call it 'snow' or 'snowflakes.'"

Tonn felt something cold forming on his arms and legs. A white substance began to coat his body. Semisolid water, his scanner read. The snow was covering Ziv, too. Her carapace glowed purple with fear.

"We're turning into snowflakes," she cried.

They were also rushing downward with the snowflakes. Despite blasting streams of hydrogen from their backpacks, they kept falling with the snow.

"Too much water has crystallized on us," cried Tonn. "We're too heavy... "

Both Tonn and Ziv, trapped inside beautiful snowflakes, fell down to the planet with a billion other snowflakes that night.

●❥

"The two aliens are somewhere in the field, but their crew can't give us a more precise location," said Will.

"Needles in a haystack," said Susan. "The best we can do is secure the area until their ship picks them up."

Green armored cars and trucks rumbled past them while dozens of soldiers ran along the edges of the field. An Army lieutenant gave a cup of coffee each to Susan and Will.

"This is good. Where did you get it?" asked Will.

"The truck stop across the road, sir," said the lieutenant, pointing at the restaurant.

Susan gulped down her coffee and turned to the lieutenant. "Secure the perimeter. I don't want anyone or anything walking into that field."

Then she turned to Will. "We don't want someone accidentally stepping on the aliens in Earth's first contact with them."

She looked at the cloud. "I was hoping that cloud would blow away, but it isn't moving. When will it snow?"

"The forecast says morning — any time now."

"The alien ship better get here quick," Susan said.

The flat sheet of snow spread as far as Tonn could see. He had never seen anything like it: nothing but whiteness everywhere.

7

"Amazing," said Tonn. "Their ground water is solid. What discoveries! The stories we can tell to our hive-fellows back home!"

"If we ever get home," Ziv grumbled. "We are stranded on an alien planet."

"But our crew is tracking the signal of our beacon." The soft beep from his backpack continued. "They will find us, and when we return home, we will be heroes."

"Hopefully, we will be alive for the celebrations," said Ziv, throwing two claws up and two claws down. She glowed bright green. "Tonn, next time trouble starts, get back inside the ship!"

Tonn flashed a pale blue in sadness. "Ziv, we will go home alive. Why not enjoy this great adventure?"

Suddenly, they heard a deafening roar from above, and a gigantic shadow fell over them.

Whats a dog doing out there?" said Susan.

A miniature dachshund, its brown coat spotted with snow, barked and ran across the field. Susan shook her head and grimaced.

"Must belong to the farmer," said Will. "We've got to get it out of there. Those aliens could be anywhere in that field. The dog could trample them."

"I know, but how do we get it out... without hurting it?" Susan looked around. Soldiers stood all around the field, armored cars sat by the roadside, a helicopter flew overhead, and still, the dachshund pranced through the snow. The Canadian Army, heroes of two world wars, was helpless against a little dog.

"Now I *really* need another coffee," she said as she began walking to the restaurant across the road. As she approached the parking lot, she read the red and yellow sign: BBQ STEAKS, RIBS, BURGERS.

*I don't need a coffee*, she said to herself silently. *I need a hamburger.*

Tonn and Ziv ran from the monster again. No matter how fast they ran, the large shadow and deep roar followed them. When they looked up, they saw a gigantic brown shape, so large that they could not see all of it. Sometimes it hovered over them, sometimes it was beside them, but it always shambled near them.

Whenever it moved, it threw giant puffs of snow into the air. Balls of snow bounced off Tonn and Ziv.

"Run fast!" yelled Tonn, his carapace glowing bright purple.

"We should have stayed in the ship!" said Ziv, switching from purple to green and back to purple again.

Then the monster ran away, and its growls became fainter and fainter.

Susan grinned as the dachshund ran towards her through the snow. Even in a weak wind, the meaty aroma of the hamburger drifted from her hand and over the field.

"Uh, the dog could be trampling on the aliens right now," said Will.

"I know, but that's a risk we'll have to take. The longer it stays out there, the greater the chance it'll step on the aliens. At least we're getting it off the field."

The dog walked to Susan and sat in front of her. It panted heavily with its tongue hanging out. The dog's brown eyes grew wide with excitement as they stared up at the hamburger.

After petting the dog's head, Susan placed the hamburger on the ground. The dog immediately began wolfing it down.

"Well, not all military projects are expensive; we solved that problem with less than ten dollars," said Susan. "Oh, by the way, I got this in my change. I remember you're a coin collector, right? Here, take it."

It was a quarter showing voyageurs paddling in a canoe, a special design for the millennium of 2000. He hadn't seen one in circulation for a decade.

"Thanks, Susan." Will smiled, and then he felt a snowflake fall on his nose. His smile faded.

"Oh, no! Is it snowing?" he said.

They looked up. Nothing else was coming down. Just one snowflake had fallen, probably blown up from the ground. It wasn't snowing yet. Still, the cloud wasn't moving away. It could snow anytime.

"We've got to prevent it from snowing," said Will.

"How can we do that?"

"Uh, move the cloud?"

"A direct approach, but there's no giant fan to blow the cloud away."

"What about taking all the water vapor out of the cloud? If we can't move it, we'll shrink it," Will suggested.

"But how can we do that?"

"A dehumidifier. I used to work for a company that sold dried fruits. They had a dehumidifier; it sucked in the air, absorbed its water vapor, and blew it back out as dry air."

"But there's no dehumidifier large enough to suck in an entire cloud. And even if we had a giant machine, how would we get it into the cloud?"

They heard footsteps crunching on the snow. Turning around, they saw the lieutenant approaching them with a small box.

"Headquarters wants photos of the first contact with an alien species," explained the lieutenant. "The General even gave me a new camera..."

Of course, thought Will. People take photos of any event: birthdays, weddings, parades, baseball games. Why not the first contact? Unfortunately, the aliens were too small to appear in the photo; historians would have to settle for photos of him, Susan, and the soldiers standing beside a snowfield.

What a shame that the aliens were so small. Ever since he was a child, he had wanted to see aliens from space. He studied biology and astronomy so he could work at the Extraterrestrial Search Center. And now, at the field where Earth's first alien visitors had landed, he couldn't see them.

"Could you please hold this, sir?" the lieutenant asked as he handed the box to Will.

As the lieutenant fumbled with the camera and a roll of film, Will saw a small white packet inside the box. He took the packet out and showed it to Susan.

"This is desiccant, a substance that absorbs moisture while the camera is in the box. It helps prevent the camera's metal parts from rusting. Maybe we can use it to absorb the moisture in the cloud."

"But how can we do that? We just can't drop tons of desiccant into the cloud. The stuff will fall right through the cloud before it can absorb the water."

"But what if we can keep the desiccant hanging inside the cloud?" said Will.

"And how can we do that?" Susan asked as the helicopter flew over them.

"Helicopters?" said Will, hearing the helicopter.

"Suspend bags of desiccant from helicopters?" she said. "It's possible, but that would use up a lot of fuel."

"There's got to be a way," said Will. He watched his breath form another small cloud and float away.

Float away...

He snapped his fingers. "Helicopters and planes aren't the only aircraft we have, are they?"

Soon after the big brown monster went away, another creature started chasing them. The new beast, a blue shape, was smaller than the first one, and it scattered less snow in its path, but it made a loud clicking noise.

The clicking scared Tonn and Ziv bright purple; it reminded them of the ferocious clicking of the warrior caste in the hive.

"You were right! Next time, I will go back into the ship when trouble starts!" cried Tonn as they fled from the blue monster.

"Or you could stay inside the ship all the time!" said Ziv.

Tonn briefly turned orange. "And miss all the excitement?"

I must be bored, thought Will, if I notice a blue beetle crawling across the snow. He tried to imagine how that beetle would look to the two aliens. The insect would probably be as gigantic to them as he was to it.

His thoughts returned to Susan. She had gone back to the air force base three hours ago. Could she really get everything they needed?

A long shadow and a droning noise floated over him. He looked up and cried out.

Three white blimps sailed towards the cloud.

"Lieutenant, may I borrow your binoculars?" he asked.

He saw hundreds of white packets attached to the blimps. *Desiccant!*

His cell phone rang. "Will Lawrence," he answered.

"Captain McNaughton here," said Susan over the phone. "I'm flying one of the blimps."

"Good work," said Will.

"Don't congratulate me until we've succeeded," said Susan, "but we got everything quickly, so luck may be on our side. First, I had to convince the General that we had an emergency. Then we had to get the Prime Minister to let us buy tons of desiccant — environmentally friendly, of course. Next, we had to find three blimps — not easy, but three balloon companies lent us theirs."

She steered her blimp into the cloud. "Okay, Will, I've got work to do. Talk to you later. Over and out."

Aboard her blimp, Susan radioed the other two pilots. "Maintain different altitudes so we don't run into each other, and be careful flying and steering with all that extra weight. And a warning — the desiccant will get heavier as it absorbs the water vapor."

She couldn't see the other two blimps through the cloud. I hope we don't crash into each other, she thought, but if this plan works, we won't be in the cloud for too long.

Seven hours later, she saw one of the blimps hovering above her. The wisps of cloud were getting thinner...

"We are saved!" cried Tonn when he saw the ship land on the snow.

Off in the distance, the ship sat, its engine humming softly, and its red copper skin glistening in the light. He could see his crew rushing through the hatch to meet him.

Ziv waved her arms at them. "We survived!"

As Tonn and Ziv clambered aboard the ship, the crew shouted with joy. Tonn had never seen his crew glow so brightly orange before.

"The Extraterrestrial Search Center received a message from the aliens," said Will, listening to his phone. "They've rescued their castaways and are leaving Earth."

Susan put the dog back on the ground and shooed it away. "What a disappointment; our first contact with an alien species, and we never got to see them."

"We would've needed a microscope, but still, it would've been nice," Will agreed.

Soon, the armored cars and trucks, soldiers, and Susan were gone. Only Will stayed behind to take photographs of the field. It might look like an empty field of snow, there were no spaceships or aliens, but it *was* the site of the first contact.

He looked wistfully into the field. If only he could have seen the aliens...

He felt a slight rush of air, as if something had flown past him. A bird? A bee? In the winter?

Something gleamed in the snow. A penny. First, the millennium quarter, now a shiny new penny. Must be my lucky day, thought Will.

Just as he bent over to pick it up, the penny flew away. Will smiled.

He had seen the aliens after all.

# Moonfuture Incorporated

## by Pat York

**K**esa thought she could hear voices through the thick, gray fog in her head. And then she realized… she was getting air! Air, sweet, wonderful air! The nightmare flashed through her mind again. Sitting with her crazy, careless Dad in the stolen Moonbuggy, his voice screaming through her Moonsuit radio, "I can't find the brakes! Where are the brakes?" over and over. The feeling of flying in slow motion out of her seat. Her father's arms flailing, nearly flipping the buggy over, trying to reach for her. Watching the buggy and her helpless father vanish over the Moon's short horizon. Then walking and walking and walking until there was no air left in the flat plastic tanks on the back of her suit.

19

Then falling face first into the soft, gray Moon dust. She took a deep, deep breath of lovely air. The fog in her head thinned and she opened her eyes.

There was light and there were three faces. Kid faces. Kid faces? "Something's wrong," she croaked through a paper-dry throat.

The shorter boy spoke, "We found you near here, lying in the dust. No Moonbuggy and no air..."

"That's not what I meant. I meant that you guys are kids."

"You're a kid too," the girl said defensively.

"That's different."

"How?" This from the taller boy.

"My dad...he made a deal with the President of Moonfuture Incorporated. He offered to do a concert at her house if she'd give him permission to bring me with him to the Moon."

"What kind of concert?" Kesa shook her head to try to clear it and realized that she wasn't wearing her helmet. In fact, they'd pulled the rented Moonsuit completely off. She lay in her gold tourist's coveralls. There was a warm cloth on her head. She used it to rub her aching eyes. "He's Jason Chili," she mumbled.

"Jason Chili... like the Chili Dogs', Jason Chili?"

It was a stupid name. Kesa had always hated it. When she lived with her Mom, which was eleven months of the year, she used her Dad's real last name... Rathbone. "Yeah, that's my dad. I'm Kesa."

"Wow," the smaller boy said.

That was the first reaction of most kids when they heard who her father was. Their second reaction was

22

either shyness or envy. Their third reaction was always greed. They would ask for free tickets to one of her Dad's Techno-light Heavybeat shows, or an autograph, or a chance to shake hands — they all wanted something. "Where am I?" She pushed up on one elbow. That wasn't too bad, so she sat all the way up. Black spots flashed in her eyes and then they were gone.

The kids wore tattered black worker's overalls. The arms and legs had been cut off short and neatly hemmed. The kids were very thin and very, very pale.

She looked around at the dome. Standard housing for Moonfuture Incorporated workers...gray foam walls, one thick window facing Earthrise, and fruit and vegetable plants hanging from the ceilings and on every spare inch of floor. Most of the foam in this dome was covered with colorful pictures of trees, the Sun, kids; and strange, gray drawings of the Moon's surface. Suddenly she went cold all over. "You live here, don't you? I mean, here, on the Moon. How do you get away with it? I read all the Moonfuture regulations on the trip from Earth. No kids allowed, no way."

The smallest boy just looked at her. "I'm Spike. The guy with the red hair is David and this is Melli. This is our dome."

"You live here all the time?" she asked again.

"Are you hungry?" David held out a candy bar. The chocolate was white and dry and looked old.

Kesa shook her head no. "Did your parents get special permission to bring you up here?"

Spike moved to the other side of the room and looked out the window. Kesa was sure he was nervous. David and Melli looked as if they would jump out of their skins. "Our parents are dead, or they're back Earthside," Spike said finally.

Kesa had never known a person her own age with no parents. She knew plenty of kids who'd been left by one parent or the other, but nobody was an orphan anymore. "So why aren't you back on Earth too? I thought that the kids of Moonfuture workers live at the Moonfuture School in Canada."

Spike made a noise in his throat. "'We at M.I. love children. And that's why we won't allow children on the Moon. Just think of the damage cosmic radiation can do to developing skin and nerve cells!'" Melli singsonged the Moonfuture employee manual. Kesa had studied it for two days while she and her Dad traveled from Earth to Moonbase Lincoln. She chuckled and nodded to show them she remembered the words, too.

"Here. Catch." David gently tossed a mug to Kesa. The mug made an odd, slow-motion arc and landed softly in Kesa's outstretched hand.

"Now toss it back," he said. Kesa tried to match David's easy toss. The china mug slammed into the foam ceiling. It left a big dent and bounced back out. Melli ducked as it flew past her shoulder and into the Plexiglas window. It hit the window with a hard smack and flew back out again. David caught it in the air.

They all burst out laughing, even Kesa. "I thought I was throwing it softly!"

"The gravity here Moonside is only about an eighth of the gravity on the Earth." Melli said. "The mug doesn't weigh here what it would on Earth, but your muscles are used to treating it the way you would there."

"Just look at your hands," added Spike. "You can see the big muscles in them through the skin. That's from a lifetime of lifting and using Earth-heavy things."

Kesa looked at her own hand and then at Melli's. It was true. Melli's hand looked impossibly thin and weak.

"Moonfuture isn't a bad company," David went on more seriously, "they mean it, about not wanting kids to get hurt. But, the way my dad explained it, Moonfuture is mostly worried about money. They figure that a kid who is born and grows up on the Moon will never be able to live on Earth again without a lot of medical help. Our muscles are right for the Moon, but not for Earth gravity. We're used to handling things that only weigh a few grams. On Earth we couldn't throw a ball right, or walk, or use a pencil. Moonfuture figures it would be too expensive to pay for the hospitals and exercises to make kids fit for Earth again once they let them grow up on the Moon."

"But we don't want to go to the Earth. The Moon is our home," Spike said firmly, "we were born here. Our folks hid us from the company so that we could be a family together. They didn't want to park their kids at the Moonfuture School."

"Virtual dinner table!" David snorted, "stupid idea. Logging onto a computer to eat dinner with your own folks!"

"Our parents did the best they could. But they didn't think it all the way through, you know?" Spike went on, "Lots of Moonfuture workers get killed every year. They don't tell you about that in the tourist books, but it's true.

A mistake with your suit or a tool..." here he shrugged and Melli let her pale hair fall over her face.

"My mom died when I was a baby," David said softly, "corrupt air supply. Melli's dad and mom went together, hit by a steel cable. Then my dad took off his helmet in an airlock. The door blew. That was last year."

Spike frowned, then went on in a harder voice, "My mom is still alive. She just wanted to go back Earthside for a visit. Only, maybe she found a better job or a new husband. And maybe she was afraid to tell the bosses at Moonfuture that she left her kid behind and would they please send him to her."

"We were supposed to baby-sit him for a few weeks," David laughed and Melli raised her head with a smile. Even Spike smiled. They looked at each other and Kesa felt her heart warm.

"Seems like you have a pretty good family right here," Kesa said to Spike. "But I don't get it. How do you eat? Where does your air come from? How do you go to school?"

The three children looked at each other with gleeful sneakiness. Melli flipped her hair and Kesa watched as it slowly riffled in a way she'd never seen on Earth. "We glean."

"Glean?"

"Sure. We use the stuff Moonfuture throws away. You wouldn't think they'd throw out anything, since it costs so much to rocket things out of Earth's gravity."

"Food that's old," David gestured with the candy bar, "broken tools, dead computers, torn Kevlar sheets from dome construction, half-empty foam canisters..."

"Our folks made us this dome," Melli said, "when we were big enough to be by ourselves. And they wired it and put in solar panels and big storage batteries..."

"And all from junk!" Spike laughed.

"But what about air?" Kesa was mystified, "and water? What about water?"

Nobody spoke for a minute. Then Spike grinned. "That's our biggest secret. You know, the Moon has water frozen under its North Pole from when it was first formed. But a few meteorites are made of ice and sometimes they hit the surface. The moon has been hit millions of times. That's where the craters come from. Our folks..." she tapped her foot on the Kevlar-plastic floor. "Our folks found ice buried right here. A big chunk, almost at the surface. They figured it was a meteorite that hit the side of this crater. It was sheltered from the Sun by a rocky overhang, so it didn't boil away. Pure, $H_2O$ water ice! They used that same rock overhang to camouflage our dome. We use the water to make air for the dome and our Moonsuit tanks and for drinking and washing."

Kesa stared blankly at them. "That's unbelievable! How can you breathe water?"

Spike shrugged, looking modest. "We didn't think it up. It was our folks. There are gobs of solar panels outside. They heat the dome and charge a big array of batteries. We put ice into a vat, then melt it, then crack it into oxygen gas and hydrogen gas with battery power."

Kesa felt her eyes get big. "Electrolysis! We did that in school this year. We were studying electricity. You stick a good conductor of electricity, say carbon or copper, to wires. Then you attach the wires to the positive and negative sides of a battery. You put the conductors in the water and it breaks the water molecules into oxygen and hydrogen molecules. We could see the bubbles of gas coming out of the water. It never occurred to me that we could breathe that stuff."

David laughed, "Hey, it's the same oxygen, no matter where it comes from. When they first built the dome, our parents pumped some nitrogen into it. The nitrogen gas just recycles. We add oxygen from our ice to make it breathable. The plants clean out the carbon dioxide we breathe out...and everybody's happy."

"We throw away the hydrogen," Melli added. "We don't need it for anything, and it can blow up pretty easily."

"So can oxygen," Kesa said.

"Yeah, but we need oxygen. We're very careful," David said calmly. "You learn to be careful on the Moon."

Melli nodded. "Our folks set it all up. We maintain it. Especially Spike. He's got a real gift for batteries and chemistry and stuff. It's exactly the same system that Moonfuture uses, only a lot smaller."

Spike got a sneaky look in his eye, "We could tell Moonfuture about this ice. They'd love it. It's a lot closer to Moonbase Lincoln than the ice they're using now. But we figure they'd kick us back Earthside..."

"Now it's your turn," Melli said to Kesa. "Why were you out on the side of our crater, miles from Lincoln with no air and no way to get home?"

Kesa winced. "You're not the only guys with parents who don't plan very well." She told them the whole, sorry story of how her Dad was determined to look at Earthrise '...without those bleedin' tour goons chatterin' at us and tellin' us what to do...' And how he stole the Moonbuggy and all the rest.

"You must be worried about what happened to him after you fell off," Melli said.

Kesa felt her face go hot and red. She hadn't even considered that her father might be hurt or lost in the great expanse of airless wilderness. "He never gets into trouble," she said weakly, "He can talk his way out of anything or buy..."

"Can't buy your way out of no air," Spike snapped. David shot him a poison glance. Spike looked stubborn, then guilty. "Sorry," he finally mumbled, "but it's true."

Kesa felt a sudden bubble of panic crawl up her throat, "He made us sneak out while everyone else was sleeping. No one saw us leave. No one will know how to follow him!"

"Sure they will," David's voice was full of encouragement. "There's no wind or rain on the Moon, nothing to destroy buggy tracks. They're probably on his trail this minute."

"But I ran out of air. He will, too!"

"Just wait a second," Melli opened a cabinet in the tidy dome, and pressed a touchpad. The room suddenly filled with voices. "We monitor all the suit radios we can. We've learned all about the different jobs people do, what they're building, all sorts of stuff."

Spike chuckled, "Yeah, like who's throwing out good garbage and where they're dumping it..."

One voice suddenly came in louder than the others, "...that's twelve klicks from the Tourist Dome. Sandi, how in blazes did he get so far?"

A loud sizzle, then a woman's voice, "He must have been going at top speed until the battery ran out. What a mess. You should see. When he tried to jump the crevasse he must have slipped. I never saw a cracked helmet in all my time here. Until now."

There was a crackle and, "...the girl?"

"No sign," the woman's voice came through, "We're guessing she fell into the crevasse itself. Recovery will be impossible — it's too deep. Even with all his money we can't afford to hunt down her body."

"What do you think it means?" Kesa asked frantically.

Three kind faces looked away from her, then back. She knew what it meant, she just didn't want to say it out loud.

"It sounds like it was fast, like it didn't hurt," Spike patted Kesa's shoulder awkwardly.

"You can get away with doing dumb stuff on Earth where the air is free and there's a hospital on every corner," David said gently, "Around here you just can't."

"He wasn't dumb!" Kesa snapped back at him. She suddenly felt furious. She wasn't sure if she was angrier at her Dad or at David. "My dad is an artist. A very creative person. Creative people don't always make plans and think carefully, but that's because their minds are on their art!"

They didn't try to fight with her, instead, they waited while she cried, sitting quietly until she was done with her first wild grief.

"This is just how I found out about my parents," Melli said softly.

"They think I'm dead too," Kesa looked up at Melli. Melli nodded, the others followed her lead.

"That means you could stay here with us," Spike said. "You could live on the Moon if you want to."

Kesa shook her head, rubbing a hand over her eyes. "It would kill my mom to think I... And anyway..."

"You must hate the Moon now," David's voice sounded very sad.

"No!" Kesa shook her head, "No, I love it here. But it's not my home. I'd miss my mom and our house and my school, and my friends."

Melli nodded thoughtfully, "That's just how we feel. We're, well, citizens."

"I know," Kesa went on gently, "I was thinking about that, and the hidden ice, and you guys eating bad chocolate for food."

"We get fresh fruit from the plants," David waved a hand defensively at the mass of green that filled the dome.

"Anyway, I was thinking that, once I get back Earthside, I could help you."

"You can't tell anybody about us," Spike said.

"Yeah, please don't, Kesa, please!" Melli added.

"I wouldn't! I never would. You saved my life!" Kesa was almost offended that they could imagine such a thing. "All I'm thinking is this... you said before that you have computer access to things from here."

David nodded, "You should see Melli. She can get anywhere. She can even write computer programs for the machines Spike puts together."

"Right. I'm figuring that if your folks could build an electrolysis machine, I'll bet they got you connected to communications here with a satellite dish, right?"

The kids nodded.

"Well, if you can pick up Moonside radio and computer signals, you can aim the satellite at Earth and pick up email from me! I have a computer at home, too. And I'm not so dumb. Maybe I can help you think up ways to live more comfortably. Like, if you have a question, you could tell me and I could ask around on the 'net until I get an answer."

"Hey," Spike's eyes lit up. "There's a better way than that! Mom's email account is still active. I check it all the time!" He blushed suddenly, set his jaw, and went on, "Well, what I mean is she hasn't sent any messages, and nobody has sent any to her. But her name and password are still active. If we don't want our satellite signals picked up heading toward Earth, the easiest way to contact you is by using her account."

"Perfect!" Kesa said. "See? Then I *can* help."

"Great!" Melli said warmly and threw an arm around Kesa's shoulder. She stepped to a desk and took out a piece of cloth to write on. "Here's the email address and a map of our location. The crater's name is here, there's the compass rose and here's where we are."

Kesa knew she could memorize the map and the address in a few seconds, but she took the cloth respect-fully from Melli and shoved it deep into one of her pockets.

"When I find out stuff you need to know, I'll put it on my website as if it were a school project. Okay?"

She told them her email and web address.

"We'll walk you over to the dump closest to Moonbase Lincoln," Spike said, suddenly shy, "and we'll watch until you get to the airlock."

"We always travel in pairs," David added, "it's safer."

"Can I come back and see you someday?" Kesa asked.

Melli held out Kesa's suit, ready to help her with the unfamiliar clasps and closings, "You'd better! But don't worry, we'll keep in touch."

"How am I going to explain not running out of air?" Kesa asked, wriggling into her suit.

"Just tell them an extra tank fell out of the buggy when you did. And that you found a second one in the dump partly full. That will explain why you're using an older model. We didn't dare refill the tank you were wearing. You couldn't have explained that!"

David went to a closet and pulled out a set of air tanks. Kesa felt him snap off her empty tanks and snap the new ones into place. "Are you okay?" he asked. "You can't...uh...you can't cry in the helmet. The moisture fogs the inside and you can't see."

Kesa bit the inside of her lip before she answered, "I'll be okay, I promise."

Melli gave her a quick hug, "Try to look surprised when they tell...when they..."

"Don't worry," Kesa thought her voice might break, but it didn't. "Whatever I do, they'll think it's normal. That's what my mom told me when my grandma died. She said everybody knows that people can act all kinds of different ways."

Kesa looked at each of them carefully before they put on their helmets. "I just met you, but I'm going to miss you. Next time I see you, you'll probably be part of Moonfuture yourselves."

David nodded firmly, "We've always been part of Moonfuture. Someday we'll tell them about it."

They checked their suit seals and their air, slowly, and carefully. Melli pulled a handle, the air lock swung open and they left the dome of the first kids on the Moon.

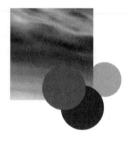

# The Word Unspoken

## by Marcel G. Gagné

Shanzi paused and looked toward the haunted city. From out here, just a short distance from the wall, it even looked haunted. Of course, all Lanky cities were haunted so this one was no different. She took a deep breath. *Come on, girl. This is no time to turn chicken.*

After adjusting her backpack, she took a sip from the canteen at her side, preparing to walk the final steps to the circular wall and its thousands of doors. She looked to the ground at her feet. The signs of time were everywhere. Weeds pushed up through cracks in the old road leading inside. Trees grew thick and branches hung low.

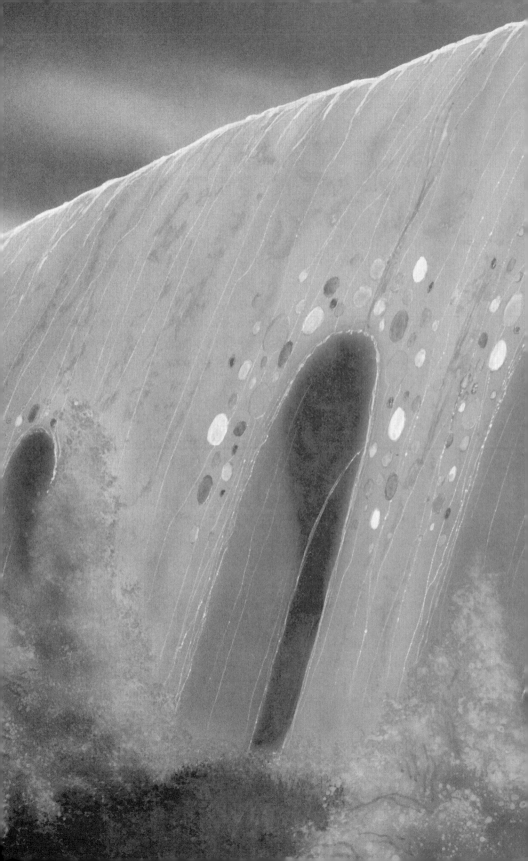

The humans who had first settled on this planet called the previous inhabitants Lankies because these people had all been very tall and very thin. The Lankies had long ago disappeared without a trace, but their ghosts could be felt in every Lanky city. For that reason, few humans ventured close. Trying to work with the feeling that some-one was always looking over your shoulder was more than most people could take for any length of time. Ghosts were everywhere, but no one had ever found a Lanky, dead or otherwise. It was one of the great mysteries on a planet full of mysteries. Nearly one hundred years after humans first settled Lank, little was known about the Lankies themselves. Humans knew them to be intelligent, scientifically advanced, and had managed a few words in their language. That was about it.

Leaves brushed Shanzi's head as she ducked to avoid a particularly low set of branches.

Crack!

Upon hearing the sound, Shanzi felt as if her heart had stopped. She could almost hear her mother now. "If you had listened to me and forgotten this nonsense, you wouldn't be lying here dead, killed by some horrible creature."

Except it wasn't nonsense. She was an archaeologist. In truth, she was a 14-year-old who had just started high school and was a long way from graduation, but she was still an archaeologist, she reminded herself. Or would be, someday. As Shanzi raised her head proudly, ready to continue with her mission, she stopped again. Had she felt something?

*Calm down,* she told herself. *You're imagining things.*

Unfortunately, telling yourself that you're only imagining things, doesn't help you with things that are real. The tiny legs creeping across her neck were that kind of real. Shanzi tried not to scream, held her breath, and quickly reached for the thing at her neck, tossing it to the ground.

The scalpel spider had fallen on its back and was desperately trying to right itself, its legs waving madly. Each of those eight legs ended in razor-sharp barbs. If any had pierced her skin, so far from home, Shanzi knew she was as good as dead. Her hand shaking, she reached around and felt her neck where the spider had landed and pulled her hand back. There was no blood. She was okay.

Meanwhile, the spider continued its fight to roll over. Shanzi grabbed a nearby branch, inched over to the spider, and with a single swing of the branch, crushed it.

As she paused, shuddering, she heard a voice.

"Ooh, gross!"

"Mixa! What are you doing here?"

Shanzi's seven-year-old sister bent down to look at the crushed spider. She grimaced. "Depends," she said.

"Depends on what?"

"It's ugly," Mixa said as though she had already forgotten the conversation.

Shanzi sighed with frustration. "Depends on what?"

"Depends on what you're doing here," Mixa said, her attention to the spider now evaporated. "Have you got any food in that backpack?"

"Of course I have food. You don't think I'd go exploring without supplies, do you?" Shanzi looked at Mixa who carried nothing. "Unlike you. You're not even dressed for it."

Before leaving, Shanzi had done her best to outfit herself for a hike. Her backpack had a phone in case of emergency but currently off, a first-aid kit, and some food. Her canteen was heavy with water. Her clothes were loose fitting and completely covered her arms and legs. Her pants were tucked into her socks so nothing could crawl in. Mixa, on the other hand, wore a yellow sundress and had a bright red ribbon in her hair.

Mixa ignored the comment. "Well, I'm exploring too." With that, she walked past Shanzi and up to the Lanky city wall. She looked to the right and left, sizing up the many doors built into the circular wall. Lanky cities were all like this, circular structures with back doors into individual Lanky homes. The 'front door,' the one that actually led into the city center, could only be accessed by walking through the house. Mixa started to head for one, stopped, picked another, and then, unable to decide on one, she picked a handful in front of her and began reciting "Eenee, meenee, minee, mo."

"Mixa!" Shanzi caught up with her sister. "Stop it and go home right now. I don't need you to trail along behind me like some demented shadow. Besides, there are ghosts in there." Shanzi crossed her arms and smiled, sure that her last statement had won the argument.

"Of course there are ghosts," Mixa said. "That's what 'haunted' means." Shrugging at Shanzi, Mixa pointed to the door directly in front of her, and yelled, "Mo!" She then walked up to the door and said, "Dra-a-ak," the Lanky word for 'open.'

*Dra-a-ak, indeed,* Shanzi thought. She clenched her teeth and followed Mixa. Someone had to keep the little troublemaker safe. Refusing to give in quite so quickly, Shanzi added, "Okay, but next time you come exploring with me, make sure you wear proper clothes!"

'Open' had been the first recorded word of the Lanky dictionary. It was discovered, according to legend, after early explorers had given up trying to enter one of the walled cities. The chief explorer had expressed his disappointment, stretching out the word in Lanky fashion, and the doors had opened. Harmless words in one language sometimes meant entirely different and even funny things in another. Kids who wanted to curse in front of their parents would claim to be speaking Lanky.

The door was tall and narrow, built for the original inhabitants who, in pictures, where all tall, spindly creatures. Like humans, they had two arms and two legs, but they stood one and a half times as tall. Adult humans entered the doors sideways. Mixa and Shanzi simply walked through.

"Just don't touch anything!" But Mixa was already gone. Sighing, Shanzi followed.

Lankies, like humans, loved to take pictures. There were plenty of them on the walls of this house. Shanzi walked up to one, and using her sleeve, wiped away the dust of years. It was a picture of a Lanky mother, father, and one child, which was kind of the usual Lanky family. Their faces were all without expression which Shanzi always found strange. Didn't these people ever smile? The strangest things though, were their eyes, which were large, flattened, oval things. Instead of a single black pupil, each eye had five vertical slits, and each slit could be a different color. The majority of Lanky eyes, it appeared, were red, like in this picture. Obviously, red was the dominant eye color. Shanzi studied them admiringly.

Like looking into a Lanky mirror, she thought.

Shanzi pictured the mainstays of every country fair, long curved mirrors with a sign above that announced, "Look like a Lanky!" Her grandmother, who had *actually come from Earth* when she was a kid, had told her once that they had mirrors like that on Earth, and that no one had ever heard of Lankies back then. Shanzi remembered thinking how incredible that was.

Then she heard Mixa scream.

When Shanzi rounded the corner, she found Mixa huddled along a hallway, looking up at nothing. Shanzi knew better. She ran to Mixa's side, feeling the touch of the invisible Lanky ghost as she reached her sister. Taking Mixa's hand, she took her to the front of the house away from the presence in the hallway.

"I ran right into it," Mixa cried.

Shanzi cradled her sister. On one hand, she wanted to comfort her, but on the other hand... "I told you not to follow me. Now, will you go home?"

Mixa wiped her eyes. "Why? Will you?"

"No. I'm staying here until I make an important discovery."

"But why?"

"Because..." Shanzi stopped herself before continuing. She didn't want Mixa to know. Heck, she didn't want *anyone* to know. With no one else around and against her better judgment, Shanzi told her. "I just got my career evaluation last week. I haven't even shown it to Mom and Dad yet. The school says I won't be able to study archaeology, that I'm not cut out for it. Me!? Can you believe it? Well, I'm going to show them by coming up with the most important Lanky discovery ever."

"We're all supposed to do what we're good at," Mixa said. "There aren't enough people yet for us to choose our own careers."

"Yeah, that's what they teach you in school. Back on Earth, people learned to do what they wanted. Even here on Lank, some people get to choose anyway. I'm going to be one of those people. Besides, there are two million people on Lank now. That's a huge number."

Mixa reached up and wiped away a tear from Shanzi's face. Shanzi hadn't realized that she too, had been crying.

"Come on, Mixa. Let's discover something together."

"What if they don't want us in the house. Maybe they want to kill us all," Mixa offered.

Shanzi groaned. "Then we'll leave the house and wander in the city. I just want to have another look around in here first. Besides, the Lankies are all dead, and the dead can't hurt the living."

"Is that true?"

"Yes, Mixa. It's true."

"That's good." Mixa followed Shanzi who wandered around picking things up, looking at them only to put them down again. Her sister seemed more interested in what was around. Mixa was more worried about ghosts. "I wish we could turn on some lights," she said. "It's dark in here."

"The lights don't work," Shanzi replied. She was turning a small glass globe over in her hands.

"Why not? The door worked."

Shanzi closed her eyes and took a deep breath. "Because the door is voice-activated. The right sound, 'Dra-a-ak,' opens it. Either the lights are all broken, or we just haven't figured out what word turns lights on. Now, do you mind? I'm working." Shanzi whispered 'sheesh,' put down the globe and picked up a Lanky book.

The book had a few recognizable words in the Lanky language. Every three or four words were followed by colored dots. No one had yet figured out why Lankies decorated their books like this. Color dot decorations were everywhere. Lankies loved to decorate things with them. Circular cities. Colored dots. What did it mean?

"Shanzi, what do you think happened to them?"

"Who?" Shanzi snapped as she put the book down.

"The La-an-kies." Mixa stretched the word out in Lanky style.

Before Shanzi could snap her reply, a presence stroked past her, or she past it. She felt a cold shiver run up her back and she grabbed Mixa's hand. "Come on kiddo, there's nothing more to see here." She almost ran to the front door, yelling "Dra-a-ak" as she neared the door, and jumped through it and into the street with Mixa in tow.

"Wow!" It was Mixa. She had not felt what Shanzi had and was instead focusing on the city before them. "Awesome! That's a huge big city! Bigger than anything people have ever built."

"The Lankies *were* people, Mixa. And it's not that big. Besides, I've been to Bezore and there are over 50,000 people there. I'll bet you can't even imagine that many people."

Mixa, unimpressed, continued to survey the streets and other houses with awe. "What did they die of?" she asked.

"Nobody knows," Shanzi said, warming to her favorite topic. "Lankies didn't preserve or bury their dead, so there are no bodies to study. No one has ever found any evidence of holocaust or plague or anything. No sign. If it wasn't for the fact that everything is haunted, people would think they had just gotten up one day, and left."

"Why do they stay around? Why don't they go to heaven?"

Shanzi shrugged her shoulders. *What was heaven for a Lanky?* she wondered. Nobody knew for sure whether they even had a religion. Maybe that's what the colored balls were for. If that was true, then the link to under-standing these people would be found in a church.

Grabbing Mixa's hand, Shanzi headed purposefully down the street. "Come on, Mixa." If she was right, then she only had a few hours before dark and, as Mixa had pointed out, nobody knew how to turn on Lanky lights. She had a small flashlight in her backpack, but it was a long way to travel back home with so little light.

As they moved through the streets, the girls zigzagged to and fro to avoid the ghostly presences they could feel but not see. They kept so close to each other that at times, they had trouble walking. Silent Lanky vehicles were everywhere. They looked new, although years had passed since the people who made them vanished. They no longer worked; at least, no one had ever been able to *make* one work.

Up ahead, squat spires rose in grotesque silhouettes against the sky. Mixa, who was trailing a few feet behind, called out, "What an ugly place! What do you think it is?" Shanzi turned briefly and caught Mixa's expression, her face twisted in revulsion.

"The books say that these were probably churches, but nobody knows for sure."

The structure was grotesque, but inviting. A semicircular panel above the door was decorated with hundreds of colored dots, looking a lot like the cards opticians used to test for color blindness.

Shanzi felt Mixa squeeze her hand tight. Her sister was more worried than she would admit. What could happen to you if you disturbed a Lanky Holy Place? They had walked a fair distance to get here and had felt many ghosts around them. After a while, thought Shanzi, it doesn't feel as bad.

"Come on, Mixa."

The two ran toward the old church, then slowed almost to a stop as they neared the front steps which they climbed carefully. The door swung smoothly open at Shanzi's voice command and closed behind them seconds later, leaving them both in twilight.

Mixa's hand tightened even more as they continued to walk. There was a massive entrance that looked up toward a high, partially translucent ceiling. She had seen some old horror movies from Earth that featured places like this. *Gothic.* Even the word was spooky. Shanzi started to shiver. Had she thought that it wasn't so bad? This was certainly starting to feel like a bad idea.

"I'm scared," Mixa finally admitted.

"You're the one who wanted to come with me."

"And you weren't supposed to come here. Nobody is."

"Enough, Mixa! Just stay close. There's nothing to be afraid of."

Mixa stopped and tugged hard at Shanzi's hand. "Why do we have to keep going?"

"MIXA, YOU ARE SO ANNOYING! *We* don't have to go *anywhere*! I never asked you to follow me and you don't have to follow me now. I'm going to have a look around." Shanzi was shaking. "You stay here, and keep quiet!"

She shook free of Mixa's hand and started to walk away. Behind her, she could hear Mixa starting to cry but she continued to walk. *It won't hurt her to cry a little,* she thought.

"Sha-a-an-zi!" Mixa cried out through her tears.

Shanzi stopped and hung her head down, feelings of anger and shame mixed in equal proportion. The voice of her conscience was giving her what for. *Mixa is just a little girl. How can you do this to her? Well, why did she follow me, then? You have no right to be here, either.* The instant of thought asked a lot of questions, but then something else happened. Some of the lights came on.

Mixa did not seem to notice, but cried out once more. "Sha-a-an-zi!" She dragged out the name in a near shriek.

Still more lights came on and as the room grew bright, Mixa abruptly stopped her crying, and Shanzi looked up in astonishment. The 'church' began to take on a different look in the light, a functional look. There were three floors above her and rooms circled the large central area. *An atrium,* she thought. *This isn't a church.*

There were benches circling a structure in the center of the large room. It had a large circular stone top with a depression in the center. To Shanzi, it looked less like an altar and more like some kind of centerpiece. But what kind? There weren't enough benches for those to be pews.

First things first. She ran to Mixa and held her sister's head against her stomach. "I'm really sorry, Mixa. I'm sorry I left you like that." She pulled back and held Mixa's face in her hands. "Do you know what you've done? You've just made an important discovery!"

Mixa wiped her eyes and smiled at that. "I did?"

Behind Shanzi, in the center of the atrium, a fountain, silent for centuries, came to life. Water rose and fell over the stone 'altar,' adding a welcome sound to an otherwise silent place.

Shanzi grabbed Mixa's hand. "Come on," she said and ran with her to the nearest room. She pushed the door open and barreled in.

"Sha-a-an-zi," she cried into the darkened room. Instantly the lights came on. "This is wonderful!" she said to Mixa. "My name stretched out in Lanky fashion means 'turn on the lights' or something. This qualifies as a discovery, and you discovered it. Do you realize, Mixa, that people have been trying to get the Lanky machinery to turn on, do something, *anything*, for years and no one has figured it out, until now?"

Mixa beamed. "But it was your name that did it," she graciously offered. "You're the archaeologist."

Shanzi looked at her sister, feeling a strange mix of guilt and joy. She wondered what important discovery she would have made on her own. Mixa might have been a pain, but it was Mixa who had shouted out her name and turned on the lights — the same Mixa she had threatened to abandon. Bending down, she kissed Mixa's forehead. "Thanks."

They rushed from room to room, skipping or running, watching everything fill with light. Finally, they ran back to the center atrium fountain and started to splash water at each other. Within the mix of giggles and horseplay,

neither noticed that there were now more than just
ghosts watching.

"Chi-i-a ze-o-o da-i?"

Shanzi spun around to face the voice, instinctively
putting herself between Mixa and the intruder. She
swallowed hard. A Lanky! A real, living, breathing,
talking Lanky! A Lanky who was right now examining
them, his head bobbing up and down and sideways.
The water from the fountain ran down her back and onto
Mixa's head, but Mixa held her place under the cascade.

"Chi-i-a ze-o-o da-i?" the figure repeated. He was a
full two meters tall, and wore a form-fitting gray suit that
made him look official. *Business-like,* Shanzi thought.

When no answer came, the Lanky official simply
stared at them, the vertical slits in his large, oval eyes
flashing in alternating colored bars; on the right, three
reds, a green, and a yellow, while the left slits stayed a
deep blue. He tilted his head and waited.

"That's how you communicate, isn't it?" Shanzi asked,
though the Lanky just looked at them. While he waited,
he spoke his original phrase of greeting, "Chi-i-a ze-o-o
da-i?," then repeated the color sequence, three reds, a
green, a yellow, and five blues.

"What does he want?" Mixa said quietly behind her.

"He's trying to talk to us, only he doesn't just use
sounds for words. See how his eyes change color? I'll
bet those are words, too."

"The colored dots in the books?" Mixa offered.
"Those are words?"

"Yes," Shanzi replied. "It's a language made up of both light and sound." Then, she had an idea. "Mixa, give me the ribbon from your hair."

Mixa pulled the red fabric away and handed it to Shanzi, who took out her flashlight and pushed the lens firmly against the ribbon. Then, she turned the flashlight on and off, ten times. Each flash was a bright red dot. After the tenth, she stopped and waited for the Lanky to respond.

All of the Lanky's eye slits flashed to red, just like in the Lanky family pictures.

"And that, Mixa, is a smile."

"Ne-e-ta me-e-rallo," the Lanky added, repeating the red-eyed smile.

Hours later, several representatives of the human population of Lank, as well as officials from the government city and language experts from the university, had arrived. Shanzi and Mixa's parents had been informed but had been asked to stay outside during these first meetings with the Lankies.

There were also several more Lankies present. Shanzi stood with the group, offering the odd word. The Lanky they had met earlier was eager for her to stay close. He kept looking at Shanzi and smiling his red-eyed smile.

"Shanzi?" Mixa called.

Shanzi turned around to look at Mixa, who sat in front of the fountain on one of the semicircular benches.

She excused herself from the Lanky official, pointing to her sister for explanation. The Lanky smiled again. "Tee-ah-sah, Mi-ix-aa."

Shanzi laughed. "Yes, Mixa." She waved and walked over to sit with her sister.

"What is it?" Shanzi said.

Mixa asked, almost whispering, "What's happening?"

"Quite a bit," Shanzi answered. "As I understand it, the Lankies didn't die at all and they didn't really leave either. Something happened to the planet a long time ago, something that was poison to them. Whatever this thing is, it happens on a regular basis, and *will* happen again. If they stay, they die. They don't know about space travel so they don't have spaceships."

"Then where did they go?"

Shanzi shrugged. "Nowhere. Not really. They have some kind of space-displacement machine. They could all go into a sort of suspended animation, like the sleepers on spaceships, like in your picture books, only they didn't really go anywhere. The machine they have opens a kind of door into another place and they all walk through it. They've been frozen there for centuries waiting for the machines to decide that it was safe for them to come out again. The problem is, something went wrong and the machines never woke them up even when it was time." She reached out her hand and grabbed Mixa's chin. "That is, until you got the machines going again. When the lights came on, all the other systems fell in behind them and the Lankies woke up." Shanzi leaned in close. "You know what? Everybody's talking like you and I are heroes. Isn't that wild?"

"So, Mom and Dad aren't going to be mad?"

"No," Shanzi said with a wide-eyed smile. "I don't think so."

Mixa looked around. There were Lankies walking around everywhere, talking, doing things. "So what happens now?" she asked.

Shanzi followed her eyes. Having grown up with picture-book Lankies, they didn't look or seem all that strange. She smiled. "I'm not sure. In fact, there's only one thing I know for sure."

"What's that?" Mixa asked.

"We're going to have new neighbors," Shanzi told her sister.

# By Its Cover

## by Isaac Szpindel

**H**arlan Stubbs was invisible. At home, at school, no matter where he went, it was as if people looked right through him. He could be seen, of course. It was just that no one ever paid any attention to him. Harlan was so completely ignored that it was like a disease or a mutation had damaged the genes that might have made him a special or noticeable person. Miserable in his condition and desperate for a cure, Harlan found himself on his own, in a strange place, and about to do something he would likely regret.

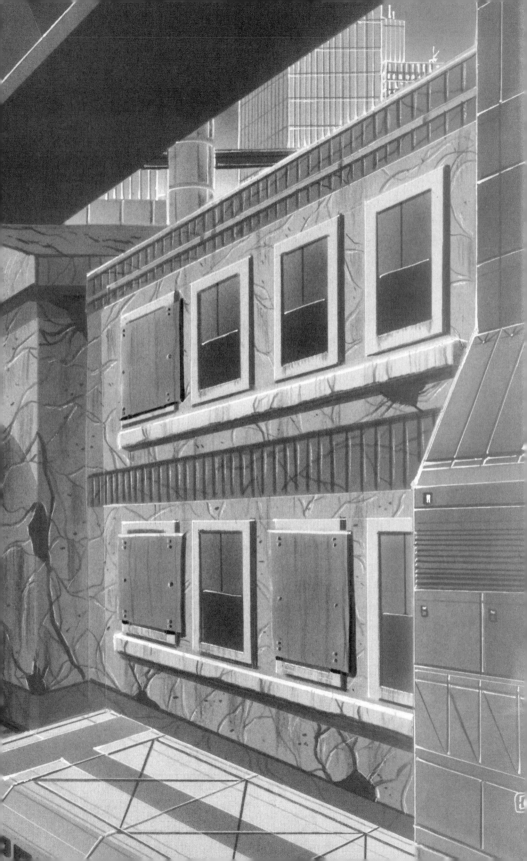

The place was an old stone building that, like Harlan, stood lost and forgotten within a lonely part of town. Its surfaces had crumbled from neglect and its windows had gone blind under thick layers of dust. Still, despite the building's haunting appearance, hope pushed Harlan into the long line of people that inched single file toward its entrance.

In line, no one spoke. Instead, they passed their time playing the latest downloadable interactives on their portables. Harlan had left his player at home, so to occupy himself he unfolded and read the flyer that his hands had almost worn beyond recognition.

> *Better Living Through Chemistry*
> **Dr. Carol Lewis**
> Personal Biochemical Enhancements
> ———
> Confidential
> ———
> Satisfaction Guaranteed

The small print underneath was no longer readable. It was the first flyer Harlan had ever seen and one of the few pieces of paper he had actually touched. It couldn't be real, he thought to himself.

The line shortened into the building. Inside, the air was dry and the light was low and artificial. Harlan noticed a musty odor, like his grandfather's clothes. The building had been a library before downloadable interactives had replaced books and before the Environmental Protection Act had outlawed paper products. All around, the walls were covered with what appeared to be old-fashioned books. Harlan had seen pictures of books on the net, but had never seen or touched a real one. They were quite dull, he imagined, just plain words on paper. He was glad he hadn't been born fifty years earlier.

"Stubbs?" A high voice startled Harlan from his thoughts. "You're next." The voice came from a small woman carrying a large digital notepad. She wore a ragged old lab coat and looked up at Harlan through glasses twice gone out of style. "You related to Harry Stubbs, the author?" she asked.

"I wouldn't know. My parents are divorced and I don't know my father's family that well," answered Harlan.

"I see," she said, disappointed. "Follow me."

The woman hurried into a small elevator. Harlan bent his tall and clumsy form in beside her. He often felt that his body had been intended for someone else. "Are you Dr. Lewis?" he asked.

"Dr. Lewis?" she asked back.

"Yeah, from the flyer." Harlan showed it to her.

She examined it over her glasses and smiled. "Look at that. That's me, all right. You were looking for someone else, maybe?"

Harlan was puzzled by Lewis' strange response. "I don't think so."

"No, well you're quite right to ask," Lewis responded. "We can't believe everything we see now, can we?"

"I guess," answered Harlan, confused.

After what seemed like an uncomfortably long time to Harlan, the doors opened onto another floor much like the previous one. Immense wooden shelves packed with books extended inward from the surrounding circular wall onto a central laboratory area. Fragments of people and movement showed through gaps in the shelves where books had been removed.

"Previous customers," said Lewis, noticing Harlan's attention. "They won't bother us."

Harlan followed Lewis through the aisles and past earlier customers on a winding route to the laboratory area. "Are they reading those...?" he asked.

"Books?" Lewis offered. "It's not a bad word, you know."

"No, but they're illegal, aren't they?"

Lewis spun on Harlan. "My flyers aren't printed on real paper made from trees," she said. "And even if real paper is illegal, books aren't. The people who passed those laws did it to protect our trees. They never wanted us to stop reading or making books. People see what they want to see and forget what's important."

Harlan wondered if his questions were offending Lewis. Despite her unusual behavior, he had nowhere else to go, and no one else to turn to.

"Would you look at that?" Lewis continued. "Now here I am losing track of what's important." She smiled at Harlan and offered him a seat by a broken metal desk. Lewis took her own seat opposite him.

"So what kind of enhancement would you like?" she asked. Her fingers danced silently across her notepad.

"Doesn't it say on your pad? I mean, I answered all the questions and transmitted them with my application." Harlan hoped he wasn't wasting his time.

"I have to make sure my information is correct, don't I?" Lewis responded.

"I want people to notice me," came Harlan's frustrated response.

"Interesting. Not terribly original, but interesting. You want people to notice you as soon as they see you? Just like that?"

"Yes," Harlan answered. Maybe Lewis knew what she was doing after all.

Lewis shot past Harlan, stopped at a laboratory table at the end of the room, and waited for Harlan to follow. On the table, an open maze surrounded a rather large sleeping rabbit. The entrance to the maze was shaped like a rabbit's hole. At the exit, a small bowl held a dried-out carrot.

"So, now that we know what you want," said Lewis, looking at the rabbit. "What do you want to do about it?" Harlan wasn't sure if she was talking to him or to the rabbit.

"I thought you might know," suggested Harlan, still puzzled by Lewis' behavior and odd choice of location.

"Would you look at that?" said Lewis, grinning again. "We do have a few options. A few things we can try, but I can only enhance one system at a time."

"System?"

"You'll understand. More than one system at a time, and the strain's too much for the body. Also, there have been occasional surprises."

"Like side effects?" asked Harlan.

"Like this rabbit. He got my muscle mixture. It should have made him even faster than he already was, but watch." She tapped the rabbit lightly on its back. It woke with a start and took off at near-blinding speed. After passing two corners, it came to an abrupt stop and collapsed.

"What happened?" asked Harlan.

"Too hard on the body," Lewis explained. "Heart and lungs can't keep up. A few turns in the maze and it's so tired it has to sleep it off."

"Yeah, but what does that have to do with me?"

"If we enhance your body, you could become a sports star. A real somebody. Famous, even."

"You can do that?"

"Not really. Not this way, at least."

"Then how about making me smart," Harlan suggested, "so I can figure out how to get noticed?"

Lewis led Harlan to another table where a large Tabby cat lazed on a short stack of books. "This is Chester," she said pointing to the cat. "Chester got my brain booster cocktail. Now, look at her."

"She's just sitting there."

"Exactly. That's what she does now. Sits there all day with that silly grin, thinks and does nothing else. I made her think more, but I couldn't make her any smarter. If I didn't feed her she'd forget to eat and her body would shut down completely." Lewis stared at the cat. The cat stared back.

"What's she thinking?" Harlan felt he had to ask.

**67**

"Now that's a good question," said Lewis, regarding Harlan with new respect. "I'll have to remember to ask her." Lewis and the cat continued their stare. Harlan wasn't sure if he should wait for a conversation to take place.

"Doctor?" Harlan finally interrupted. "How about my problem?"

"Oh yes, of course," she said, returning her attention to Harlan. "Let me see, now. Your skin. We could do something really outrageous to your skin." She picked at him like a tailor measuring a suit.

"Does it have to be outrageous?"

"It will get you noticed. Decorating the skin with tattoos and piercing used to be quite the rage, you know."

"Sounds painful."

"Sure, but reversing it, that's even more painful. Also, people get used to it, so it only works for a short time."

"Is there anything less drastic?"

"Skin pigmentation changes. We could turn you any color, really. Takes time, though, and weakens the skin. Makes it easier for germs to get in and infect the body. And forget about going out in the sun. How about green? Very soothing. Easy on the eyes, you know."

Harlan was desperate, but so far Lewis hadn't offered any reasonable solutions. "Is there anything safer?" he asked.

"In what you're looking for? I'm afraid not."

"Nothing?" Harlan was crushed. Lewis, he thought, was his last chance.

"I do have something, but it's experimental," said Lewis, raising her eyebrows.

"Any side effects?" Harlan was almost too afraid to ask.

"Unpredictable. Mostly, it works or does nothing at all."

"Sounds like it's worth a try," said Harlan.

"Also, I seem to be missing one ingredient," Lewis admitted.

"What is it?" Harlan knew there had to be a catch, the experiment sounded too good to be true.

"If I knew, it wouldn't be missing."

"I guess it couldn't hurt," said Harlan, trying to sound brave. Realistically, he had no other choice.

"Okay then, let's get started." Lewis disappeared through a wooden door behind one of the tables. Harlan heard some crashing sounds, the squeal of a tap turning, and the sound of a container filling. Lewis emerged moments later carrying a dusty test tube full of a clear liquid. "The instructions are on the label," she said, holding it out to Harlan.

"'Drink me?'" Harlan read the label aloud.

Lewis nodded excitedly. "Fluids get absorbed directly. None of that messy digestion in the mouth and the stomach."

Harlan hesitated, tipped the tube into his open mouth, swallowed, then wiped the dust away from his lips. The liquid tasted exactly like water.

Lewis circled Harlan and inspected him. It looked like she was waiting for something to happen. Suddenly, she pulled him into a hug and pressed her ear tightly against his chest.

"What are you doing?" asked Harlan, shocked by Lewis' unexpected closeness.

Lewis didn't answer, but released her hold.

"Did you do something to my heart?" asked Harlan, thinking that an enhanced heart might improve both his strength and his endurance. He could become an athlete without the rabbit's nasty side effects.

"You could look at it that way," answered Lewis in her usual peculiar manner.

Harlan followed Lewis back to her desk. There, she set her notepad aside and searched through the clutter that covered its surface. Some of the paper she was sifting through, thought Harlan, must have been real.

"Now, as to the issue of your payment," said Lewis, still rummaging through her desk.

"I have some money saved up," offered Harlan.

"Not like that. You're an experimental subject, so I can't charge you. You'll be helping with my research instead," said Lewis continuing her search. "Besides, we are still missing that unknown ingredient and I do have a guarantee." Finally, she slid a yellowed card out from under the mess and offered it to Harlan. It contained some written words and a long code of numbers and letters separated by a decimal point.

"I've never seen anything like this," said Harlan.

"It's an index card," Lewis said. "We do things here the old-fashioned way."

"What things?" asked Harlan suspiciously.

"Good old-fashioned research. Book research," said Lewis with an air of satisfaction.

Harlan was less than impressed. "But that'll take me ten times as long and be a hundred times more boring. Isn't there an interactive version of this stuff?"

"Sure, but it's not quite the same. My research requires imagination, and this particular problem, your problem, requires a very special kind of imagination. Those interactives are full of other people's imaginations. Books let you use your own."

"I don't know if I can. I mean, I've never read one before."

"Good, an open mind. The code on the card will help you find what you're looking for."

Harlan turned the card over in his hands. "It could take me weeks to read just one book." He could tell by the expression on Lewis' face that she had little sympathy for him.

"Would you look at that?" said Lewis, glancing at her bare wrist. "I have people waiting. Come back when you've found what you need." She waved Harlan off and disappeared into the shelves.

It didn't take long for Harlan to realize that the code on his index card corresponded to labels on books and to guides on the surrounding shelves. As he searched for the match, he passed by other customers, alone and in pairs. None of them paid any attention to him.

After a few wrong turns, Harlan came to a long row of similar looking books. There, the code led him to the far end, where he quickly realized that he had company.

She was about Harlan's age, and like Harlan, she seemed to be searching for something. Her face was thin and delicate, and her hair, dark and long. She stood more than a head shorter than Harlan, stretching from the tips of her toes, trying to get a better view of the top shelf. She was uncomfortably close to the area in which Harlan was searching. Sensing either his presence or his discomfort she turned to him and smiled. Harlan felt his face go hot.

"Are you helping with Dr. Lewis' research?" she asked.

Harlan nodded, but couldn't manage to speak.

"Me too. My name's Julie."

"I... I'm Harlan," he stuttered.

"Nice to meet you, Harlan."

"Me too," said Harlan. And in an effort to excuse his nervousness, "I'm not used to books."

"Me neither," said Julie. "They don't look like much on the outside and they're full of words on the inside."

"Yeah, a lot more work than an interactive." Harlan was feeling more at ease. Someone else, at least, felt the same way he did.

Julie kept her eyes on Harlan and smiled. "Do you need any help?"

"No. I think I can manage." Harlan wished he had said the opposite.

"Oh," said Julie, disappointed. "I could use some help."

"I'm not very good at this," said Harlan, fumbling again.

"Actually, you're perfect." Julie pretended not to notice Harlan blushing and pointed to the top shelf. "Mine's up there," she continued. "I went back to tell Dr. Lewis I couldn't reach it, but she just acted like she already knew and said I'd get what I came for, eventually."

"I can do that for you," said Harlan, finally able to express himself properly.

"Great. I'll help you find yours after we get mine. It's up on the top shelf, third from the end." She handed Harlan her card. He looked it over for a moment, then held his own up beside it.

"Is something wrong?" asked Julie.

"I don't know. I think they're the same," said Harlan, handing both cards to Julie. He could feel his heart beating harder.

"What should we do?" asked Julie.

Harlan couldn't answer. His breath was coming too quickly and his heart was beating too heavily for him to speak.

"We could try to read it together. If you want to…" Julie suggested, shyly.

Harlan could only manage a short reply. "I'd like that." He could feel the blood rushing up to his face again, so he turned away from Julie and slid the book off the shelf. It was thick and dusty and it gave off the same musty odor that Harlan had noticed when he had entered the building. After he felt like himself again, he handed the book to Julie.

"Looks long," she said, stopping to blow the dust off its jacket. "I hope you have plenty of time."

"Lots," said Harlan between breaths. Then, after a moment of consideration, "What about the missing ingredient? Do you know what to look for?"

Julie held the book close to her chest. "No, not really. But I'll bet we can find it together."

Something told Harlan that she was right. "I'll bet," he said, repeating Julie's words. "Want to go somewhere? You know, to read?"

Julie nodded her agreement. Harlan noticed, for the first time, that she was blushing as well.

Together, they made their way through the maze of books and shelves to the elevator. Once inside, neither spoke. Harlan lost himself in thoughts of Julie, books, and strange experiments.

The elevator descended to a stop and opened its doors on the ground floor. There, Harlan noticed the difference immediately. A change was occurring. The people in line were starting to pull themselves out of their interactives. They were looking up and watching Harlan and Julie leave. Harlan suspected they were staring at the book in Julie's arms, but before long he realized it was something else entirely and then, somehow, it didn't seem to matter.

# Rain, Ice, Steam

## by James Alan Gardner

The old man was out there again in the rain. Big fat drops were coming down hard — a real summer downpour that banged on the roof of Kate's camper van like buckets of marbles tossed from the sky. But there he was… the little old fellow in his shabby, brown coat, kneeling in the mud by the side of the river.

With the sheets of rain falling so thick, Kate couldn't see much of what he was doing — bending over the riverbank, putting something into the water. Was it a glass jar? Yes, it looked like he was dipping a jar into the fast-flowing current, letting the jar fill with the muddy water that rushed and foamed as the rain flooded down.

But why would anyone want water from dirty old Bell's River? Everyone knew the river was polluted by acid rain and pesticide run-off, not to mention all those factories upstream that kept bragging how much cleaner they were now than twenty years ago. Maybe they had cut back on the amount of waste they dumped into the water, but the river still wasn't clean, was it? There were "No Fishing or Swimming" signs everywhere you looked, and on a hot summer day when it wasn't raining, the water stunk like something that had died.

Kate stared at the old man again. He was getting up now, jamming a cork or something into his jar to close it. As he tucked it into his coat pocket, Kate thought to herself, Maybe he's some kind of scientist. Maybe he's taking samples of the water to see how polluted it really is.

But if that was the man's job, it sure was a lousy way to earn a living on a day like this. His brown coat was soaking wet. His shapeless, white hat was drenched through too, dribbling streamers of water onto the old guy's gray hair and down his neck. Just the sight of it made Kate shiver as she imagined the rainwater squishing through the man's clothes with every step he took.

**80**

She watched as he walked up the narrow path from the river to the gravel road. He moved slowly with his head hunched down; the path must be slippery with all the rain, and the old man obviously had to be careful where he stepped, keeping his eyes on the mud. The man didn't even see the truck racing down the road toward him... but Kate did.

Kate recognized the truck — a big, blue pickup that belonged to Blind Dougie. Of course, Dougie wasn't really blind... people had given him that nickname because he was a terrible driver who didn't pay enough attention to the road when he was behind the wheel. Dougie raced past Kate's camping spot a dozen times a day, always too fast and bouncing wildly every time he hit a bump. This time, Kate couldn't tell if Dougie even saw the old man on the path; the truck roared by without slowing down, spraying the man with a hail of mud and gravel.

The old man fell. He didn't get up.

Kate had a first aid kit in the camper: a very complete kit, because at one time she'd considered becoming a paramedic. That hadn't worked out...just like all the other jobs Kate had toyed with. She'd gone to university thinking she'd do something with computers; then she switched over to history; then a year studying drama; then a summer when she sent out a dozen applications to teachers' colleges, but nobody accepted her and that was all right because she didn't want to be a teacher anyway.

The truth was that Kate didn't need to work at all — her family had tons of money, and she'd inherited a trust fund big enough to live off for the rest of her life — but she hated just hanging around with nothing to do. Eventually, she'd rented this van and found a spot to camp far away from everything so she could get her head together. While she was here, she thought she might try to make paintings of the landscape...or write a movie screenplay...or maybe learn the guitar and develop a singing act...

She never imagined she'd end up slopping through the rain to help some man she didn't even know. But it looked like that's what she had to do. Heaving a sigh, Kate grabbed the first aid kit and an umbrella, then slid open the camper's side door.

There was a huge puddle right outside. She tried to step over it, but didn't quite get far enough. Her foot splashed down into rainwater that immediately soaked through her sneaker. Grumbling under her breath, she slopped across the wet grass to see if the man was hurt.

Even as she approached, the man struggled to his feet. He looked a bit wobbly, but Kate was happy to see he could still move under his own power. "Are you all right?" she shouted against the rattle of rain on her umbrella. "If you want to sit down for a bit, you can come to my camper."

The old man didn't answer. In fact, he took a few quick steps away from Kate, then stumbled on a pothole in the road and nearly fell down again. "Hey," Kate said, rushing forward to help him keep his balance, "you should really come back with me. Just till you're feeling better. I'll make you a cup of tea, and maybe in a few minutes, the rain won't be so heavy."

She'd put one arm around the man's shoulders to hold him steady. Now he shook her off; he was a lot stronger than he looked. Maybe he wasn't as old as Kate thought — he could be one of those men whose hair turns gray when he's still fairly young. Without thinking, Kate shifted her position to get a better view of him...

The man threw up his hands to hide his face and sprinted off into the bush.

Kate gaped after him in surprise — not just because he'd run away, but because of what she'd seen in the split second she'd had a clear look at him. Blind Dougie's truck must've kicked up a stone that hit the man hard in the forehead. The stone had gashed open a cut that dribbled out blood...and the blood had been solid jet black.

It wasn't hard following the man's path through the woods — the ground was so muddy, his footprints stood out quite plainly. There was plenty of light too; it was two o'clock in the afternoon, and despite all the rain clouds blocking the sun, Kate could see perfectly well.

Yes, it would be easy to track where the man had gone...
Kate's only question was why she was so keen to do it.

She told herself she had the best intentions: if the man
was seriously hurt, she shouldn't let him run off into the
forest by himself. But Kate knew that wasn't the real
explanation — she was out here because of that black
blood. Maybe it had just been a trick of the light, but if
it wasn't...if his blood really was black...if he wasn't a
man at all but some strange creature that hung around
here, far from all humans except Kate's camper and
Blind Dougie's shack up the road...

If any of that was true, Kate knew she was crazy to
be chasing him. She'd watched plenty of horror movies;
it was stupid to go off on your own, following some
monster. But for the first time in her life, Kate finally had
something to *do* — something important that had
dropped right into her lap. How could she just go back
to her camper and pretend nothing had happened?

Three minutes ago she was just a bored, twenty-five-
year-old rich kid with no purpose to her whole existence.
Now...now she was an idiot, chasing after a monster or
an alien or something, and for all she knew, she could
end up dead.

She kept following the tracks anyway. If she ran
away from this, she'd hate herself for the rest of her
boring, pointless life.

After ten minutes of following the path, Kate found that the footprints led into a cave: a hole that disappeared straight down into solid limestone. She knew there were dozens of unexplored caves in the area; that was one of the reasons she'd decided to camp in this out-of-the-way spot. Now and then, she'd wondered if she might like to be a cave explorer — yet another idle fantasy, imagining herself bravely venturing underground, discovering prehistoric cave paintings or huge crystal caverns never before seen by human beings. Kate had even taken a cave-crawling course last winter while she was in France... two days of poking around "beginner caves" in the Pyrenees.

So Kate had learned a bit about caves — enough to know you should never go into one without an experienced partner. It was totally insane to consider climbing down into this hole on her own, following a man whose blood was black. But she just couldn't bring herself to leave the man alone; this might be the closest she'd ever get to doing something extraordinary.

There was caving gear in her van — she'd brought it with her, in case she found herself in the mood for subterranean adventure. Kate ran back for it as fast she could: a lot of rope, a tough leather jacket that would protect her from scraping against sharp stones, and a helmet with a light on the front. She also took her first aid kit, just in case the man (or whatever he was) truly needed help. Then, very carefully but filled with excitement, Kate returned to the cave and lowered herself inside.

For the first little while, she could see the man's muddy footprints on the cave's stone floor. But the spots of mud slowly dwindled as the man's boots wore themselves clean, and by the time Kate got to a fork in the tunnel, she couldn't tell which way he'd gone.

She decided to take the left fork...and she used a big piece of chalk to mark an arrow on the wall pointing back to the cave's exit, so she could find her way out again. Then she crept quietly up the left tunnel.

It was cold down here in the cave — much colder than the summer day outside. When Kate exhaled, she could see her breath...and the farther she went, the colder it got. After a while, she was sure the temperature had to be below freezing; here and there, she could see slicks of ice on the rock walls. Good thing she was wearing the leather jacket! But it was strange this place was so chilly. In the cave-crawling course she'd taken, the instructor said caves might be cool at the top but they usually got warmer when you went deeper down.

Now that she was underground, Kate's only source of light was the one attached to her helmet. Soon, however, she realized she could see more light up ahead — bright but orange-colored, shining from around a curve in the tunnel. Quickly, she turned off her own light so she wouldn't be seen; then she moved cautiously ahead, until she could peek around the corner.

She found herself looking down on a small chamber with two tunnels leading out of it — not a normal cavern with rough, uneven walls, but a room that had been dug out cleanly from the rock. The floor of the room was some distance below her; the tunnel she was following came out high up one wall, like a third-storey balcony overlooking a little courtyard. It gave her an excellent view of everything down on the floor...including the old man right in the middle.

He was sitting slouched over at a metal table, his back toward Kate. In front of him stood the glass jar he'd filled with river water. It was only half full now; he'd obviously poured the other half into a second jar that was sitting on what looked like a small, stove burner.

The water in that jar was bubbling and boiling, with steam pouring out the top. From time to time, the man glanced at it but did nothing. He seemed to be letting the water boil away completely, leaving behind a layer of ugly sludge in the bottom of the jar. Some of that sludge would be harmless mud, stirred up naturally as the river current flowed...but the rest would be the foul-smelling results of the river's pollution. Factory wastes. Pesticides. Heavy metals. Acids and poisons and who knew what else.

Kate wondered if she'd been right all along — maybe the man *was* a scientist studying pollution. But normal scientists didn't build secret labs down in caves. They also didn't have jet-black blood.

She waited quietly, breathing as little as she could. When all the water had boiled out of the glass jar, the man pressed a button on the tabletop. *Turning off the stove*, Kate guessed. With a great sigh, the man picked up the jar with his bare hand and went out one of the tunnels in the side of the room.

*Ouch*, Kate thought. The man didn't show any pain at all, grabbing a boiling hot jar straight off the burner... which was one more indication he might not be a man at all. At least not a human one.

Ten minutes later, he had still not come back to the room. Kate was getting cold — even her leather jacket couldn't keep her warm against freezing temperatures. And it *was* freezing down here. There was still half a jar of water on the table below, and Kate could see a thin layer of ice forming on its top.

She could also see how cloudy and dirty the water was, almost brown with mud and pollution. The sight of it made her sick — she had known Bell's River was in terrible shape, but hadn't realized how bad until she saw the man's two jars: one with the pure water boiled away, leaving behind ugly sludge, and the other freezing solid so you could see all the filth that was trapped in the ice. "Like something you'd see in a science museum," she whispered to herself. "Ice so dirty, everyone can see how awful it is."

"You are correct," said a voice behind her.

She whirled around. The old man had crept up behind her without making the tiniest bit of noise. He stood in front of her now...and even in the dim light, Kate could see he was *not* a man at all. His face was far too puckered, covered with odd bumps and ridges that made it look like the bones of his skull were completely different from a normal human being. The skin on his cheeks was inhuman too, scaly and slightly orange. When she'd seen him before, he must have been wearing a mask or special make-up; otherwise, she would have recognized immediately that he was some unearthly creature.

Surprisingly, she wasn't afraid of him. Perhaps it was because he had a big bandage on his forehead where the rock from Blind Dougie's truck had hit him. The bandage was tied very clumsily, the way a little kid might try to do it while playing doctor. Kate just didn't feel scared of anyone who did such a sloppy job of patching himself up.

"I wish you hadn't followed me," the man said. He spoke with a strange sort of accent, unlike anything Kate had ever heard. "I don't know what I'm going to..." His voice cut off as a shudder went through him.

"What's wrong?" Kate asked.

The man's hand fluttered up to the bandage on his head. "I think I'm bleeding again," he said. Then he fell forward into her arms, unconscious.

He wasn't heavy to carry — not nearly as heavy as a real human being. Kate managed to pick him up and lug him back up the tunnel until they reached the fork again. This time she went down the right hand side; soon she found herself in the little room where she'd watched the man boiling his water. She set him in the chair and tried to make him comfortable. Then she got out her first aid kit to see what she could do.

When she took off the awkward bandage he'd put on himself, Kate saw that the man had been right. He *was* bleeding again. Bleeding a lot. In humans, a tiny head injury can bleed so much you think it's worse than it really is; but Kate suspected the man's wound truly was serious. It looked very deep...and maybe the stone had broken some of the strange underlying bone structure. Black blood kept spilling from the gash, even after Kate taped fresh gauze over the wound.

"You need to go to a hospital," she said, even though the man was still unconscious. "I'm sure you won't want to, but if that cut doesn't stop bleeding..."

She stepped back for a better look at her bandage-work. It would do; she'd give it five minutes, then check to see if the bleeding had slowed down. If not, she really would have to get him to a hospital — whatever he was, she couldn't let him die.

In the meantime, she wondered if there was anything else down here that might be useful in treating him. If this guy was an alien (and that was the most likely explanation), he might have a super-science medical machine that could heal any injury with the push of a button. He might also have some fancy communicator to call for help from Alpha Centauri...or some high-tech weapon Kate should take away so he couldn't decide to shoot her. Whatever might be hiding in this cave, Kate wanted to find it; and with the man unconscious, she'd never have a better chance.

There was a second tunnel leading out from the small room. Kate headed down it, and soon could see the dim glow of artificial lights ahead of her. Whatever the old man was, he had a fantastic setup down here, with electric lighting and all this space carved out of stone...

Kate stopped, dumbstruck, as she came to the doorway of another room. It wasn't a small chamber like the one she'd just left — this new place was huge, the size of a full hockey arena built deep underground.

And the chamber was filled with jars.

Shelves and shelves of them, all carefully stoppered up and labeled with squiggly writing that didn't look like anything on Earth. To the right, the jars held chunks of ice; to the left, the jars were empty except for deposits of dried sludge in the bottom.

"Wow," Kate said softly. "Wow."

There had to be thousands of the jars...maybe millions. How long had it taken to collect all these samples? Kate had seen the man twice before today, both times in the middle of rainstorms. If he came out of his cave every time it rained and filled up a single jar with river water, how long before he collected so many water samples?

Years. Centuries.

Kate walked slowly forward, trying to take it all in. On the nearby shelves, the chunks of ice looked dirty and brown; the jars with dried sludge gave off a nasty chemical smell. But as she went farther along the rows, the ice grew clearer and the smell slowly faded. "Like going back in time," she whispered, "to the days when the river was clean." Of course, there was always some mud in the water — a bit of dirt was perfectly natural. But Kate had no trouble distinguishing between ordinary mud and the ugly stuff that poisoned the water now.

"So," said a voice from the door of the room. "What do you think of my collection?"

The man was standing in the doorway...or more accurately, he was leaning there, supporting himself against the wall so he wouldn't fall over. "I've been collecting a long time," he said. "Five thousand of your Earth years."

"So you're not from Earth yourself?" Kate asked.

"No. I'm from... elsewhere." He waved his left hand over his head, gesturing vaguely toward the sky.

"Why are you here?"

"To study. I'm a researcher and historian. When I came across your planet all those years ago, I thought it would be interesting to see how you...developed."

He lifted a jar that he'd been holding in his right hand. Kate recognized the chunk of brown polluted ice inside — it was the jar that had been put out to freeze on the table in the other room.

"This is what your world has come to," the alien man said. "Or rather, this is what's happened to the river I've been watching for five thousand years. Some rivers are better; many are worse. It's been educational to track your race's...progress.

"But," he went on, "I've been here long enough." He touched one hand to the bandage on his head. "I need to go home and get this fixed. Anyway, in the past few years I haven't enjoyed my work very much. I used to love the rain, but now...I don't like it a bit. I *hate* the kind of rain you get here." He shrugged. "So I'll pack up my samples and take them all with me — then analyze exactly what poisons you people are dumping into your water systems...and your atmosphere...and the soil..."

"But you've spent five thousand years here," Kate said. "How can you walk away now? That's just giving up. And isn't the river getting better? People claim the water is cleaner now than twenty years ago; if that's true, you shouldn't be such a pessimist, and if it's false, we should tell the newspapers or something so everybody knows the clean-up isn't working. Don't you want to *do* something instead of just quitting?"

The alien man didn't answer right away. Finally, he sighed. "I don't know if the water is cleaner or not. I haven't analyzed my results — all this time I've been gathering samples, and I haven't a clue what I've got." He lifted his hand to his head again. "But I have to leave. Head injuries are very serious in my species. And once I'm gone, the study is over, isn't it? I've kept it going for five thousand years, never missing a single rainfall... but I don't have a choice. I can feel that I'm still bleeding."

"Look," Kate said, "you go home and get yourself fixed. If it rains again while you're gone, I'll fill in for you. I've got plenty of spare time and I've seen what you do — take a sample, boil off the water in one jar and freeze the other. That's easy; anybody could do it."

The man stared at her for a moment, then lowered his head. "You don't understand. I can't just fly home and fly back. When I go to my spaceship, I'll have to freeze myself in stasis so I don't die immediately. Then the ship has to fly home on autopilot...which will take *years*. Space travel isn't the way you humans portray it, zipping from star to star; the universe is huge and spaceships take a long time to get anywhere. Even if I go and come back as fast as I can, by the time I return you'll be an old woman. Do you want to spend your whole life just taking my place?"

Kate felt like she'd been hit in the stomach. Her whole life? Up here in the woods, doing nothing but playing with water jars every time in rained? That was crazy.

But what else was she going to do with her life? She'd wasted so much time on stupid stuff, taking course after course at school without committing to anything...and she certainly had enough money to support herself while she waited for the alien to return. It was completely, totally ridiculous to give up years and years of her life on a spur-of-the-moment promise to a strange creature she didn't even know; but if she didn't do *this*, what *would* she do?

"I'll take care of everything," she told the alien. "Really, I can do it. I'm standing here in the middle of the most amazing scientific study ever conducted on this planet. I mean, five thousand years...I'd like to keep that

going. And things are just starting to get interesting. Don't you want to see whether we humans solve our pollution problems? It would be a shame to throw away five thousand years of sample-collecting when there are big changes ahead. Good changes or bad changes, don't you want to see how it turns out?"

The alien took a deep breath, then let himself sag against the wall. "I want to argue with you," he said, "but I'm not strong enough." He stared Kate straight in the eye. "You're making a serious promise. I hope you're strong enough to keep it."

He reached into his shabby old coat and pulled out a small metal box. "See you in about thirty years," he said. Then he opened the box and pressed a black button inside. Immediately, the huge cavern was filled with a hard yellow light, so blazingly brilliant Kate threw her hands in front of her eyes to shut out the fierce radiance.

When she lowered her hands, he was gone. She was alone with the silent shelves of jars. *My life's work*, she thought. *These are now my life's work.*

It was very, very strange...but she was excited to be part of it all.

Outside the cave, it was still raining — not the heavy downpour it had been, but the kind of soft, steady rain that seemed as though it might never stop. She could picture it drizzling down from the sky, loaded with all the poisons that rise into the atmosphere as smoke; she could also imagine rain running off the land and into the rivers, carrying with it all the poisons people had dumped into the soil.

Maybe someday that would all change: maybe everybody would take responsibility for cleaning up the world, no matter how hard it might be. Or maybe it would just get worse and worse, as people ignored the warning signs and continued to live stupid, wasteful lives.

Either way, Kate intended to live up to her promise. She would fill a jar from the river each time it rained, keeping a record of whether humans saved themselves or ruined their world forever. It was good to be part of something big: a project to show aliens what Earthlings were like, good or bad. And maybe if someone like Kate could devote herself to a cause, it would prove that other people could too; humans weren't all selfish pigs who only cared about their own lives, but they could think about others...

With his truck's engine roaring, Blind Dougie zoomed by on the road in front of her. His front tires hit a big pothole filled with filthy, muddy water; a huge wave of spray flew up and splashed Kate hard, drenching her to the skin. Her hair was soaked with muck, and she could feel the dirt all over her face.

Dougie drove on without noticing. Kate wiped the dirt off her face, then went to the river to fill up a jar.

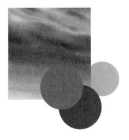